JUL 2019

For Neeve, who calls me Mama
and for Daria, who taught me
to be magical.

Mama's Cloud by Jessica Williams

© 2018 Jessica Williams
www.jessicawilliamsonpaper.com

Published by: All Write Here Publishing
Visit our website at www.allwriteherepublishing.ca

ISBN:
978-1-7753456-1-9   Paperback edition
978-1-7753456-2-6   Hardcover edition
978-1-7753456-3-3   Electronic book

Illustrations by Mateya Ark
Book design by Jessica Williams

First Edition: June 2018
10 9 8 7 6 5 4 3 2 1

Mama's Cloud

Written by Jessica Williams
Illustrations by Mateya Ark

When Mama smiles, her eyes twinkle like a
thousand fireflies. Her hair is soft and smells like
purple lilacs blooming in spring.

Mama is 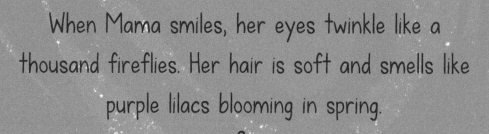 Magical.

Her kisses heal my scrapes and bumps.
When I'm sad she pulls me onto her lap and
hums to me and I can feel my sadness disappearing.

We play Fairies and Wizards and
Superheroes,
and together we always
save the day!

Mama's smile spreads from cheek to cheek.
It lights up the room and everyone around
her smiles back.
But sometimes Mama can't smile.

Sometimes a dark cloud drifts into the room and settles over her.

I don't know where it comes from,
but when it finds her the
light in her face disappears.
It takes away Mama's Magic.

When the **cloud** comes, I don't know what to do.

So I will be a Fairy.

I will float into the room on a warm breeze smelling of sunshine and lemonade. I'll use my magic wand to surround the **cloud** with sparkles.

The sparkles will
soak into the **cloud** and break
it into a million tiny droplets of water and dry them up. Mama will
smile again, and I'll sit on her fingertip and kiss her on the nose.

But I'm not a fairy and I don't have a magic wand.

So I will be a 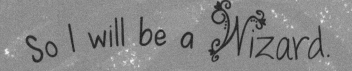Wizard.

I will stride into the room holding my gnarled staff, my long robes trailing behind me. I will wave my staff in the air and summon a giant, glittering dragon. He will swoop in and circle the ceiling, staring at the cloud with his gleaming black eyes.
The dragon will blast his mighty dragon fire and

Mama's **cloud** won't

stand a chance.

Mama will hug me, scratching my glittering dragon under the chin, and her smile will light up the room.

But I'm not a wizard and I don't know how to summon dragons.

So I will be a Fan Dancer.

I will spin into
the room and flip my
fans in a mystical dance from
a faraway land. My feet will
tap and click on the floor as my
fans spin faster and faster
in their swirling show.

Their twirling will create a beautiful tornado that will grab Mama's **cloud** and carry it from the room. Mama and I will link arms and twirl around and around the room in our happy dance.

But I'm not a fan dancer and I don't know the steps.

I will fly into the room in my secret disguise and satin cape. With my hands on my hips and my head held high, I will bravely land next to Mama's **cloud**. I will squint my eyes and use my Super Vision to blast through the **cloud**. The neon laser beams will shoot holes in the **cloud** until nothing is left holding it together. Mama will run to me and throw her arms around me. She'll call me her hero and we will fly through the window into the bright sunny day.

But I'm not a superhero and my eyes don't shoot laser beams.

So I will be an Inventor.

I will build a
machine with gadgets
and levers and pulleys
and springs. At the push
of a button the machine will whirl into action and the spinning fan blades
will blast Mama's **cloud** out of the house. Mama will smile and hug
me as she marvels at my incredible invention.

But I am not an inventor and I don't have an amazing machine.

So I will be the Sun.

I will glide to earth from the sky, all the way down to our house.

Shutting my eyes tight, I will glow with all my strength and fill our house with my brilliant light. Mama's **cloud** will burn away like the early morning fog. Mama will put on her sunglasses and come outside, her smile shining even brighter than my rays.

But I'm not the sun and I don't know how to burn away fog.

So I will be a Unicorn.

I will softly
walk into the
room bringing with
me a peaceful calm.
I will close my eyes and
lay my white muzzle on
Mama's lap. My magical
golden horn will begin to glow. A
soft, gentle light will fill the space and a glittering
mist will float up, encircling the cloud and spiriting it away.
Mama will smile and lean her forehead against mine, petting my
soft, silky mane.

But I'm not a unicorn and I don't have a magical golden horn.

I am not a fairy, or a wizard, or a fan dancer
or a superhero, or an inventor, or the sun, or a unicorn.

I'm only me.

But Daddy and Grammie and Gramps say
I have more Magic in one hug than any of those things.

So I am Me.

I walk into the room in my sweatshirt
and slippers. I sit next to Mama and wrap my
small arms around her and I tell her I love her.
And I hold her until she can be a fairy,
or a wizard, or a fan dancer, or a superhero,
or an inventor, or the sun, or a unicorn.
When I hold Mama and tell her I love her,
a little of the light begins to come back
to her eyes,

and I can see a small twinkling of her Magic
peeking through her cloud.

CPSIA information can be obtained
at www.ICGtesting.com
Printed in the USA
LVHW071923221118
597978LV00019B/475/P

9 781775 345626